"I Am Not A TELEVANGELIST!"

The Continuing Saga of Reverend Will B. Dunn

DOUG MARLETTE

Longstreet Press, Inc.
Atlanta, Georgia

For Marianne, Terry & Will

Published by
LONGSTREET PRESS, INC.
2150 Newmarket Parkway
Suite 102
Marietta, Georgia 30067

Printed in the United States of America

1st printing, 1988

Library of Congress Catalog Number 88-081795

ISBN 0-929264-00-2

Design by Paulette Lambert

Revelations

The Congregation

KUDZU
Pubescent Poet

REV. WILL B. DUNN

Our Hero

NASAL
World-Class Wimp

MAURICE
Kudzu's Main Man

VERANDA
Future Game Show Hostess

DORIS
Kudzu's Chocoholic Parakeet

MAMA
Kudzu's Keeper

TAD
Veranda's Little Brother

IDA MAE
Geekette

MR. GOODVIBES
Village Secular Humanist

UNCLE DUB
Last of the Good Ol' Boys

In the beginning,

Reverend Will B. Dunn was just a simple country preacher tending his flock . . .

a modern minister profoundly in touch with the needs of his congregation . . .

a comforting presence
at their weddings . . .

6

their funerals . . .

and their
Baptisms . . .

*a sensitive counselor
who mended their
marriages ...*

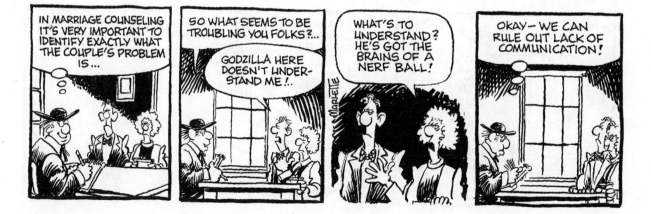

a contemporary cleric with a flair for spectacle . . .

who remained humble . . .

even when called into the glamorous world of

Prime
Time
Religion

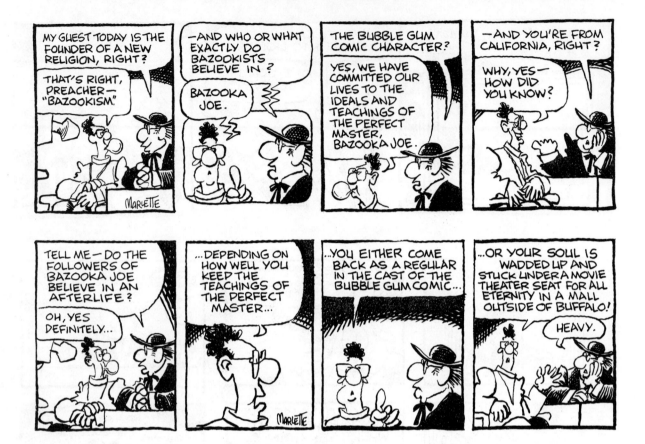

Faith

vs.

Reason

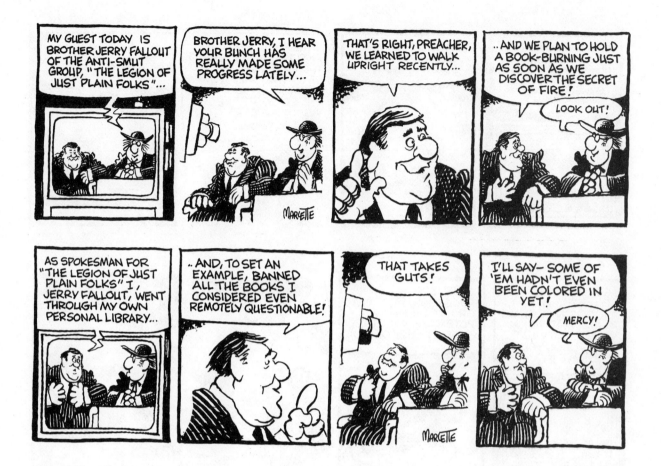

21

HELLO— I'M JERRY FALLOUT OF THE "LEGION OF JUST PLAIN FOLKS" AND WELCOME TO...

The Teen Plague

29

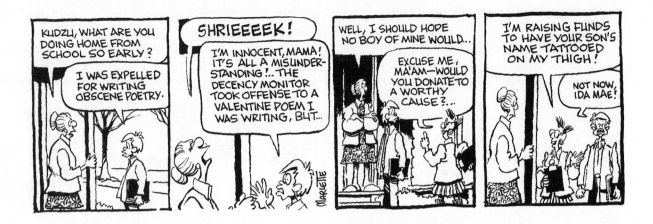

VERANDA TESTIFIES BEFORE THE ATTORNEY GENERAL'S PORN COMMISSION...

IT'S TRUE, SIR— I RECEIVED A LOCK OF CHEST HAIR IN A VALENTINE!..

‡GASP!‡

‡BLUSH‡

APPALLING!

THANK YOU, DEAR... YOU'RE A BRAVE GIRL FOR STEPPING FORTH TO REPORT THIS LEWD AND DEGRADING ASSAULT UPON YOUR PERSONHOOD...

THE CARD WAS KINDA CUTE...

..WE MUST PUT A STOP TO THESE ANONYMOUS OBSCENE VALENTINES BEING SENT THROUGH THE MAILS!...

OH, IT WASN'T ANONYMOUS—

..IT WAS KUDZU DUBOSE.

SHRIEEEK!

I SUPPOSE THIS RULES OUT GETTING A VALENTINE FROM VERANDA.

VERANDA'S TV TESTIMONY SHOCKS AMERICA...

Bypass Bugle

PORN PANEL CENSURES DUBOSE POEM

LOCAL DEB CLAIMS VALENTINE ASSAULT

GASP!

ATTORNEY GENERAL EDWIN MEESE URGES "SEVEN/ELEVEN" STORE MANAGERS TO REFUSE TO SELL "SLURPEES" TO KUDZU...

ELEVEN

..IN A RADIO ADDRESS THE PRESIDENT AND FIRST LADY ADVISE TEENS ON HOW TO HANDLE OBSCENE VALENTINES...

JUST SAY... UH...

"NO!"

"NO!"

..MEANWHILE, THE VILIFIED YOUNG POET SEEKS COMFORT AND COUNSEL FROM HIS SPIRITUAL ADVISER...

REPENT!

SUBPOENAED BY THE MEESE PORN PANEL TO DEFEND THE CONTROVERSIAL "CHEST HAIR VALENTINE" KUDZU BECOMES A SYMBOL OF ARTISTIC FREEDOM...

MAILING CHEST HAIRS IS PROTECTED BY THE FIRST AMENDMENT!

ACLU

NORMAN LEAR:

BAD TASTE IS NO CRIME IN AMERICA!

PEOPLE FOR

HUGH HEFNER THROWS A FUND-RAISER AT THE PLAYBOY MANSION IN THE YOUNG POET'S HONOR...

DEFENSE FUND

..UNFORTUNATELY, KUDZU ISN'T INVITED...

‡SIGH‡

..HOWEVER, A GOOD TIME WAS HAD BY ALL!

THAT HEF—WHAT A WILD MAN!

THE NATION IS POLARIZED BY THE INFAMOUS CHEST HAIR VALENTINE...

RADICAL FEMINISTS AND RIGHT-WING PULPIT-THUMPERS FORM AN UNEASY ALLIANCE IN PROTEST...

BAN PIG POETRY!

AMEN!

ONE TALK SHOW HOST AT FIRST SUPPORTS KUDZU...

I MAY NOT AGREE WITH HIS VALENTINE, BUT I WILL DEFEND TO THE DEATH HIS RIGHT TO SEND IT!

HELP ME OUT, LADIES!...

..BUT PRESSURED BY FEMINIST CRITICS, HE LATER RENOUNCES HIS MASCULINITY...

I WEEP FOR MY GENDER!

..AND IN A SYMBOLIC GESTURE OF SOLIDARITY, SHAVES HIS CHEST!

HELP ME OUT, LADIES!

MEANWHILE, NASAL T. LARDBOTTOM DISCOVERS NEW DATA:

ZOUNDS! HE'S INNOCENT!

SUBPOENAED BY THE PORN PANEL, KUDZU IS INTIMIDATED AND BROW-BEATEN AND IS ABOUT TO SIGN A CONFESSION...

BUT-BUT I'M NOT A COMMUNIST PORNOGRAPHER!...

THAT'S WHAT THEY ALL SAY!.. SIGN!!

SUDDENLY—

STOP! HE'S INNOCENT!

NASAL T. LARDBOTTOM BURSTS IN, QUICKLY SETTING UP HIS LATEST SCIENCE FAIR PROJECT...

.. AND LAUNCHES INTO A DAZZLING DEFENSE OF KUDZU...

..SO YOU SEE, PANEL, KUDZU NEVER SENT VERANDA A CHEST HAIR!.. EVERYBODY KNOWS HE HAS NONE TO SEND!

OUR FRIEND, THE FOLLICLE

I SUBMIT HE SENT HER A SYNTHETIC FIBER PLUCKED FROM HIS CHEST WIG!

HA HA HAH HA HA HA

THANK YOU, NASAL!

NASAL'S SCIENCE FAIR PROJECT EXONERATES KUDZU:

FAMOUS FOLLICLE FOUND PHONY

LOCAL TEEN NOT MAN ENOUGH FOR OBSCENITY RAP

HOW EMBARRASSING!

HEY—THEY SPELLED MY NAME RIGHT!

THANKS A LOT, NASAL!...

NO THANKS NECESSARY— FOR A DISCIPLE OF WILL B. DUNN, LIVING FOR OTHERS IS PAR FOR THE COURSE!

SPEAKING OF WHICH— I GOTTA GO WAX PREACHER'S CAR! 'BYE!

≤SIGH≥

MEANWHILE...

HMM...BROTHER ORAL MADE THE COVER OF "STEEPLE"!...

Steep

"YOUR MONEY OR MY LIFE!"

Oral Oral: God's Hostage

The Shrine of Bypass

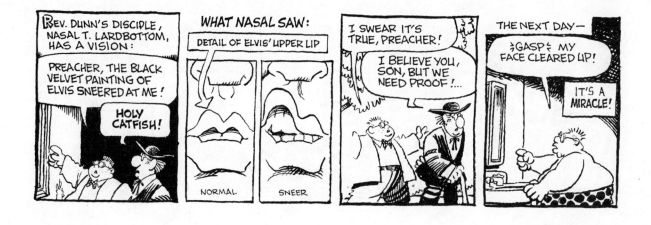

"THE SHRINE OF BYPASS" HITS THE TABLOIDS:

IRRATIONAL ENQUIRER
ELVIS SNEERS FROM BEYOND THE GRAVE
LIZ WEDS UFO ALIEN

CELEBRITIES STEP FORWARD TO VOUCH FOR THE SHRINE'S AUTHENTICITY...

I RAN INTO ELVIS ON THE ASTRAL PLANE AND HE SAYS IT'S HIM ALL RIGHT!

THANK YOU, MISS MACLAINE.

AN AD HOC COMMITTEE OF NOBEL LAUREATES DEBUNK IT AS SUPERSTITIOUS NONSENSE:

HORSE FEATHERS!

CA-CA-!

HOG WASH!

NOTED SECULAR HUMANISTS AGREE:

STUDIES SHOW IT'S ALL DUE TO LACK OF SELF ESTEEM!

MR. GOODVIBES

...YET SOME DOCTORS OF MEDICINE TURN TO THE "MIRACLE OF THE BLACK VELVET ELVIS" AS A LAST RESORT!...

TAKE TWO ASPIRIN, VISIT "THE SHRINE OF BYPASS" AND CALL ME IN THE MORNING!

NOTED SECULAR HUMANIST NATHAN GOODVIBES INVESTIGATES THE SUPERNATURAL CLAIMS OF THE "SHRINE OF BYPASS"...

POPPYCOCK!

CAMOUFLAGE!

THE GIG IS UP, PREACHER! I'M EXPOSING YOUR LITTLE SCAM IN THE NEXT ISSUE OF "PSYCHOLOGY TODAY"!

LOOK! ELVIS CURLED HIS LIP AT YOU!.. OH, DARN—YOU MISSED THE MIRACLE AGAIN!

THE GOODVIBES PROBE IS PUBLISHED—A DEVASTATING EXPOSÉ, FULL OF UNDENIABLE FACTS, IRREFUTABLE LOGIC AND THOUGHTFUL ANALYSIS!...THE NEW YORK TIMES REPRINTS IT ALONG WITH AN EDITORIAL CONDEMNING RELIGIOUS CHARLATANS...

ATTENDANCE AT THE "SHRINE OF BYPASS" SKYROCKETS!...

THANK GOD FOR SECULAR HUMANISTS!

ELVIS SHRINE TEESHIRTS

MIRACLE MUGS

EVERYBODY WHO'S ANYBODY IN SOUL BUSINESS MAKES THE COVER OF "STEEPLE" MAGAZINE!...

Steeple
PTL
JIM AND TAMMY
LOSING IT

PASS THE LORD... PRAISE THE AMMUNITION.
REV. JERRY FALLOUT

Brother Oral Oral
GOD'S HOSTAGE
"YOUR MONEY OR MY LIFE!"

REV. ERNEST ANGST
"LORD, HEAL MY TULIP!"

...AND IN THE TOPSY-TURVY WORLD OF MASS MARKET SPIRITUALITY THE "SHRINE OF BYPASS" HAS MADE WILL B. DUNN A SOMEBODY!...

LIFT YOUR EYES HEAVENWARD... SUPER!

IS MY NOSE SHINY?

THE "SHRINE OF BYPASS" COPS A COVER FOR THE PREACHER...

Steeple
REV. WILL B. DUNN
MIRACLE ELVIS CUSTODIAN

HOT DANG! NOW I GOT THE NAME RECOGNITION TO REALIZE THE HUMBLE DREAM OF EVERY TV PREACHER:

...TO BECOME COMMANDER-IN-CHIEF AND LEADER OF THE FREE WORLD!

QUACK!

BUT NOT IF SECULAR HUMANIST NATHAN GOODVIBES HAS HIS WAY!...

HELLO, BYPASS BUGLE?... I HAVE PROOF THAT THE "ELVIS MIRACLE" IS A PHONY!

SECULAR HUMANIST NATHAN GOODVIBES DIGS UP PROOF THAT THE "MIRACLE OF THE BLACK VELVET ELVIS" IS PHONY!

IT'S NOT EVEN ELVIS!

IT'S A PORTRAIT OF LOCAL "ELVIS LOOK-ALIKE" HOMER LICKSPITTLE!

'AT'S ME ALL RIGHT — I SAT FOR IT!

MEANWHILE AT THE BYPASS OPENING OF THE ANDY WARHOL MEMORIAL TOURING EXHIBIT AT THE AMERICAN LEGION HUT:

¿GASP? LOOK! THE PRINT OF MARILYN IS — IS CRYING!

¿SNIFF?

IT'S SHEDDING REAL TEARS!

IT'S A MIRACLE!

I BETTER WARN PREACHER!

...BUT THE PREACHER HAS BIGGER FISH TO FRY:

HI — I'M WILL B. DUNN AND THE LORD WANTS ME FOR PRESIDENT!

AMERICA DISCOVERS A NEW ICON:

IRRATIONAL ENQUIRER

WARHOL PRINT WEEPS

WARHOL'S MARILYN

VATICAN PROBES "MIRACLE MARILYN"

ELVIS OUT, MARILYN IN

NATURALLY, THE BLACK VELVET ELVIS SHRINE IN BYPASS IS HISTORY!...

SHRINE OF BYPASS

ELVIS MIRACLE MUGS TEE SHIRTS

...CROWDS DWINDLE, TOURISM DECLINES!...

LOCALS TRY TO PUT THE PUBLIC'S FICKLE WAYS IN PERSPECTIVE...

THE AMERICAN PEOPLE HAVE AN INSATIABLE LUST FOR THE NEW AND BIZARRE!...

...AND AN ATTENTION SPAN OF NANOSECONDS!

...SO NOW I'M STUCK WITH A WAREHOUSE FULL OF ELVIS FLY SWATTERS!

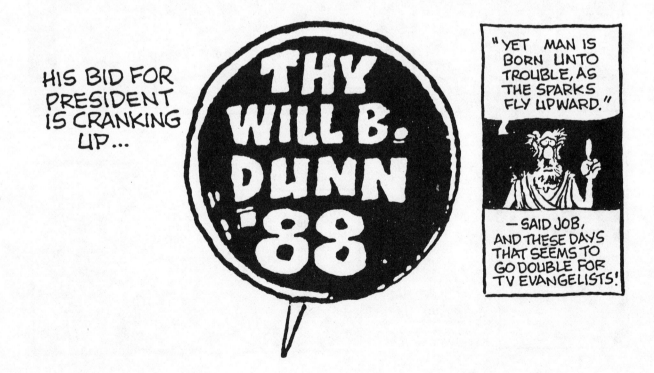

46

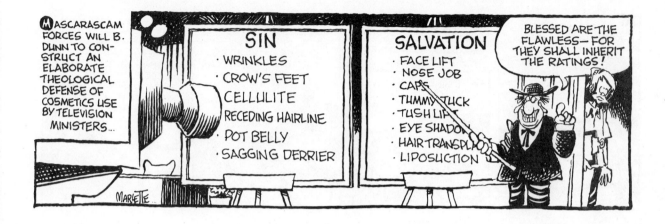

MASCARASCAM FORCES WILL B. DUNN TO CONSTRUCT AN ELABORATE THEOLOGICAL DEFENSE OF COSMETICS USE BY TELEVISION MINISTERS...

SIN
- WRINKLES
- CROW'S FEET
- CELLULITE
- RECEDING HAIRLINE
- POT BELLY
- SAGGING DERRIER

SALVATION
- FACE LIFT
- NOSE JOB
- CAPS
- TUMMY TUCK
- TUSH LIFT
- EYE SHADOW
- HAIR TRANSPLANT
- LIPOSUCTION

BLESSED ARE THE FLAWLESS— FOR THEY SHALL INHERIT THE RATINGS!

MASCARASCAM TAKES ITS TOLL ON THE FAITHFUL:

VIDEO FLOCKS FALL AWAY IN DROVES:

HOLY CATFISH! THE CBS MORNING SHOW PASSED US IN THE RATINGS!

DISILLUSIONED VIEWERS TURN TO OTHER TV FAITH ALTERNATIVES:

I INVITED GOMER PYLE INTO MY HEART!

PRAISE THE HUXTABLES!

EVEN REV. WILL B. DUNN'S LOYAL DISCIPLE, NASAL T. LARDBOTTOM, QUESTIONS AUTHORITY...

NASAL, FETCH ME A BIG MAC!

STICK IT, PREACHER!

" THE ONLY WAY TO RESTORE TV RELIGION'S CREDIBILITY..."

...IS TO HOLD A TV PREACHER ARM-WRESTLING INVITATIONAL AT CAESARS PALACE IN VEGAS!

DALE

... EXPLAINS A 900-FOOT *TRIGGER* TO DALE EVANS IN A WILL B. DUNN DREAM!

WELCOME TO **CAESARS PALACE** AND THE TV PREACHER INVITATIONAL ARM-WRESTLING FINALS...

...A CHANCE FOR FEUDING TELEVANGELISTS TO EVEN OLD SCORES, SETTLE DOCTRINAL DIFFERENCES, AND MOST IMPORTANTLY... ANSWER THE QUESTION:

"WHOSE SIDE IS THE ALMIGHTY TRULY ON?"

TONIGHT IT'S THE "WEEPING WONDER OF WOE", TAMMY FAYE BANKROLL VERSUS "THE MIGHTY MITE OF BYPASS," REVEREND WILL B. DUNN!

IS THIS A GREAT COUNTRY, OR WHAT?!

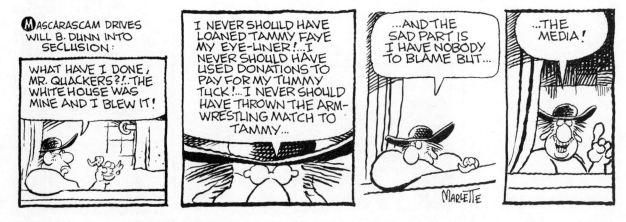

52

Render Unto Caesar

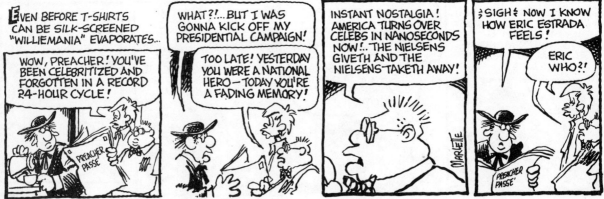

Will Power

68

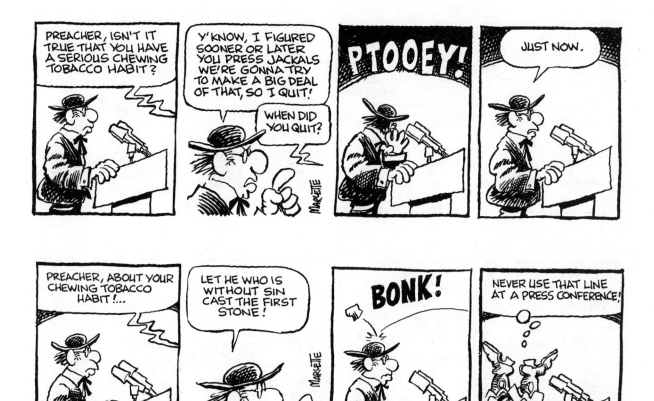

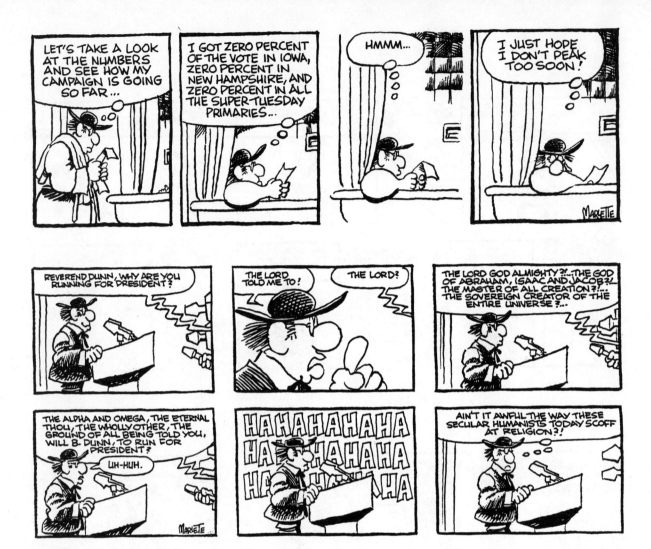

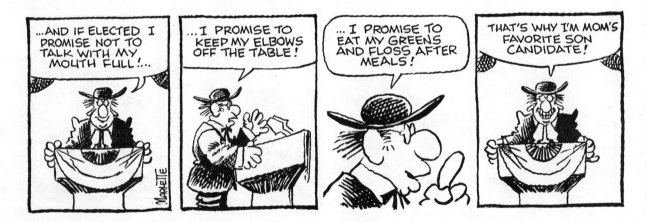

WILL B. DUNN ON:

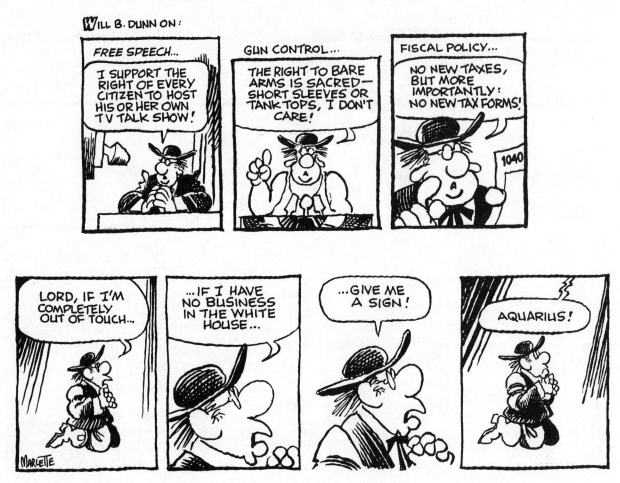

Holy War Is Hell!

90

Elvis Himselvis!

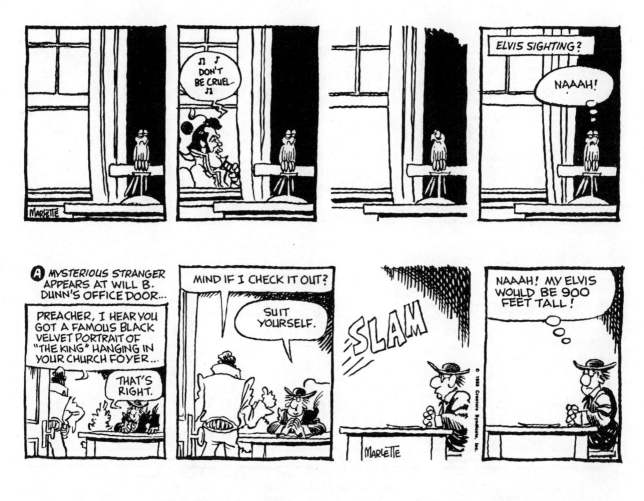

Give Us the Willies!

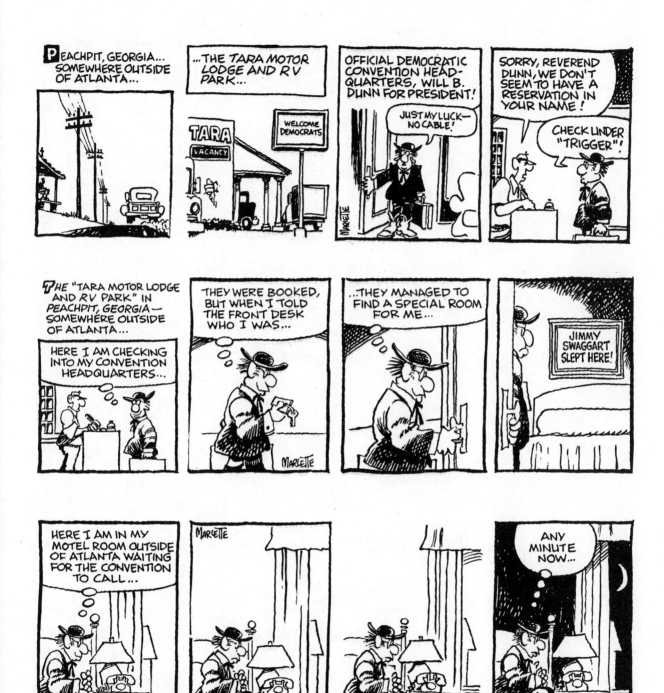

NEW ORLEANS: WILL B. DUNN AGREES TO MEET WITH GEORGE *BUSH*:

REV. DUNN, I HOPE YOU UNDERSTAND THAT ORDINARILY THE VICE PRESIDENT WOULDN'T GIVE YOU THE TIME OF DAY...

ELEVATOR

...BUT HE KNOWS WHAT A DISRUPTIVE FORCE YOU AND YOUR INVISIBLE ARMY COULD BE HERE AT THE CONVENTION...

...AND HOW EMBARRASSING IT WOULD BE IF YOU WERE ASSOCIATED WITH THIS PARTY IN ANY WAY WHATSOEVER!

I GOT 'IM RIGHT WHERE I WANT 'IM!

THAT'S RIGHT, DAN — THE VICE PRESIDENT IS MEETING NOW AT HIS HEADQUARTERS WITH REV. WILL B. DUNN...

...TO WORK OUT A COMPROMISE AND AVOID ANY DISRUPTION OF THE CONVENTION...

...SO FAR NOBODY KNOWS WHAT PROMISES THE PREACHER IS EXTRACTING FROM THE BUSH CAMPAIGN...

...AND UNCONDITIONAL AMNESTY FOR *TELEVANGELISTS*!

JEEPERS!

WILL B. DUNN WRANGLES GOP CONVENTION PRIME-TIME TO MAKE AN ANNOUNCEMENT:

MY FELLOW AMERICANS, I HAVE CHOSEN MY RUNNING-MATE...

HE HAS NAME RECOGNITION, CHARISMA, AND BRINGS BALANCE TO MY TICKET...

HE'S KEPT A LOW-PROFILE IN RECENT YEARS ON ACCOUNT OF HIS BEING DEAD...

FRIENDS, MY RUNNING MATE AND THE NEXT VICE PRESIDENT OF THE UNITED STATES: *ELVIS PRESLEY!*

MARLETTE

VOTE WILL "OF GOD"!